The Library Book

GABBY DAWNAY *Illustrated by* IAN MORRIS

T&H

There is a special place for books,
A place they live in shelves and nooks.

From A to Z stacked high in piles
These books go on for miles and miles...

So come inside and take a look
It's time to find your favourite book!

For quiet places full of books and keen or reluctant readers everywhere.
(And Ruben, who inspired this story.)
– G.D.
For Tilly, I hope you achieve all your goals, dreams
and aspirations through any adversity.
– I.M.

First published in the United Kingdom in 2021 by
Thames & Hudson Ltd, 181A High Holborn, London WC1V 7QX

This paperback edition published in 2022

The Library Book © 2021 Thames & Hudson Ltd, London

Text © 2021 Gabby Dawnay

Illustrations © 2021 Ian Morris

British Library Cataloguing-in-Publication Data
A catalogue record for this book is available from the British Library

ISBN 978-0-500-66015-7

Printed and bound in China by Shanghai Offset Printing
Products Limited

Be the first to know about our new releases,
exclusive content and author events by visiting
thamesandhudson.com
thamesandhudsonusa.com
thamesandhudson.com.au

Too many books to pick just one...
The trick is choosing – that's the fun!

No need to hurry, there's no rush
But don't forget to whisper –

Shhhhhh...

Now here is Zach and there is Ro...
You coming, Zach?

But Zach says...

No!

I don't like books.
I really don't.
I will not read them – no, I won't!

Hey Zach, why don't you follow me?
There are so many books to see...

So many books to see, it's true...
There must be one that's right for you!

A story waits inside each book,
Just turn the pages – look, look, LOOK!

I don't like ANY books, says Zach,
I want to go – please put them back.

You can't have seen them ALL, says Ro,
Why don't you have another go?

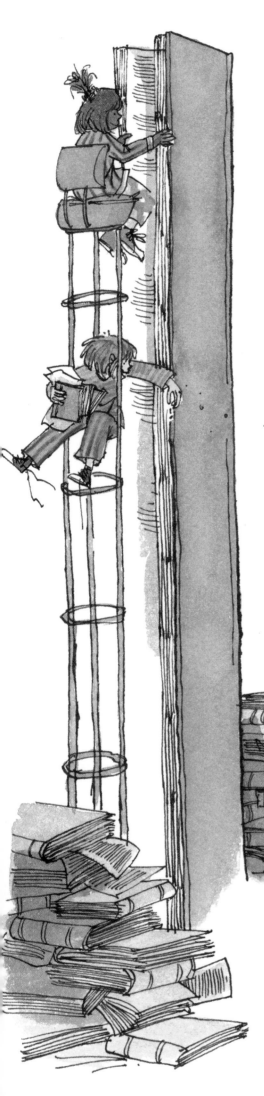

Some books are **l o n g**,
Some books are **short**,
You need to find your favourite sort!

I think you'd like a **FUNNY** story!
A thrilling tale... or something **gory**?

No, says Zach, ALL books are boring.
When I read, I end up snoring.

But have you tried **adventure books**
With **superheroes, cops** and **crooks**...?

Or **ancient legends**, **pirate** tales
With **buried treasure**, **sharks** and **whales**?

Too many words, **too many** pages...
Reading one will take me AGES.

I don't like books!
Why can't you see
These silly books are not for me?

But books make stories come alive
Just open up and in you'll dive...

These comics, poems and picture books
All wait like paper fishing hooks...

To reel you in – and with a tug
You've gone and caught
the reading bug!

I do not want to read a book,
I do not want to take a look.

I do not like books –
put them BACK!

I want to watch TV, says Zach.

But there are books on **dinosaurs**
With **scary** claws and **snappy** jaws...

Or **fairytales** with smart princesses
Slaying **dragons**, wearing dresses!

Books on **spiders,**
snakes and **lizards...**

Books on **witches**,
Books on **wizards**!

Read a book and you will find
That **MAGIC** grows inside your mind...

A book could help you banish plastic,
Save our planet – how fantastic!

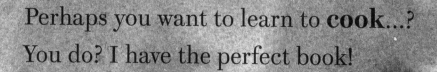

Perhaps you want to learn to **cook**...?
You do? I have the perfect book!

I'd like to learn some fancy kicks!
Is there a book of football tricks?

There is! Or you could fly through **space**,
Right here within this quiet place
Of print and pages, words and ink,
A room where you can stop and think...

So many stories everywhere!
A world of words that **we can share**!
So much to **read**,
So much to **learn**,
So turn the pages, turn – turn – turn!

So choose a book – come on, let's go!
You coming, Zach?
But Zach says...

No!

These books are COOL – don't put them back!
I want to read them ALL! says Zach.

You CAN, says Ro, and here's the trick...
You get to BORROW books you pick.

No need to rush, no need for speed
Just don't forget to whisper...

Shhhhhh, says Zach,

I want to **READ**...